Whiffy Wilson

the wolf who wouldn't wash

Caryl Hart   ORCHARD   Leonie Lord

KU-175-992

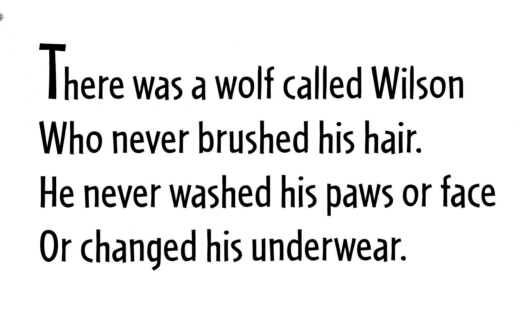

There was a wolf called Wilson
Who never brushed his hair.
He never washed his paws or face
Or changed his underwear.

He ate his dinner with his paws

Then wiped them on his clothes.

"No way!" growled Whiffy Wilson,

And then he ran away.

Wilson grabbed his teddy bear
And hid in next-door's shed.

He found a pile of coal sacks

And made himself a bed.

"I'll be as wild as a wolf should be,
Until I'm all grown up."
Then he poked his finger up his nose –
He *was* a mucky pup!

Early in the morning,
Whiffy Wilson heard a noise . . .
It was Dotty, Wilson's favourite friend
Looking for her toys.

"Eeeeuuw! What a stink!" cried Dotty,
as she rummaged in the shed.

"EEEEEEEEEK!"

she shrieked,

"A MONSTER!
SNORING IN
ITS BED!"

"A monster?! Where?!" yelped Wilson, leaping in the air.

"It's you, you twit!" said Dotty. "You gave me such a scare!"

"I'm not a monster!" Wilson whined,
As he scratched his hairy belly,
"I'm only living here because
My mum says I'm too smelly."

"We'll soon fix that,"
beamed Dotty,
And she marched him
down the path . . .

Up the stairs she dragged him,
And plonked him in the bath.

She poured in steaming water,
And scrubbed him with a mop.

. . . face!

"That's better," Dotty smiled at last,
Hauling Wilson out,

Then she wrapped him in a dressing gown . . .

and kissed him on the snout!

"Come on!" she said, "Let's play outside . . .

. . . I'm making garden stew.
Grab that stick and stir it up!
Ooh, what a smelly brew!"

They made a mudslide down the hill,
They swung from tree to tree,
Till Wilson gasped, "Oh Dotty!
We're as grubby as can be!"

"That's just perfect," Wilson beamed.
"Being mucky is all right!

As long as I can have a bath
And wash it off at night!"

So, Wilson learned the difference
Between bad dirt and the good.
He started washing twice a day,
Like every good wolf should.

His parents were delighted
And how this story ends
Is with Wilson feeling lucky
Having such a clever friend.